*Celebrate Your Love With*
# Susan Polis Schutz

"In high emotion . . . the reigning star is Susan Polis Schutz."
**—Time**

"Susan Polis Schutz remains one of the most popular poets
in America today, and her work touches virtually everyone."
**—Associated Press**

"My own favorite words of love are by a young, nationally
known poet, Susan Polis Schutz, and her husband, Stephen
Schutz. It is a collaborative effort of her words and his art.
She talks of real love as meaning 'sharing' rather than
'controlling' each other's lives."
**—Letitia Baldridge, syndicated columnist,
*Los Angeles Times***

"One picks up Susan's poetry and reads it to the quiet and
tasteful accompaniment of Stephen's art and suddenly you
are with friends you want to know and to speak with more."
**—*Saturday Evening Post***

"Susan Polis Schutz's popularity can be attributed to her
ability to verbalize intimate, honest emotions shared but
unsaid by most people. Her ability to write simply and
honestly of the deepest emotions and the most fragile and
fleeting moments strikes a responsive chord with readers."
**—*Woman's Day***

"A poet of the heart."
**—*Family Weekly***

Books by Susan Polis Schutz

*To My Son With Love*

*To My Daughter With Love*

*I Love You*

Also edited by Susan Polis Schutz

*Mother, I Will Always Love You*

*Don't Ever Stop Dreaming Your Dreams*

Published by
WARNER BOOKS

# CONTENTS

## To My Father, with Love

Dad, I want you to know
that I love you.
You are a very important part of my life.
Our relationship,
our memories and moments shared,
and the love you've given me
are all so very precious to me.
I count my blessings
to have a father like you,
and I hope you realize
that you have always been my inspiration.
You have guided me in each decision
and encouraged me to reach
for every dream.
You have helped me,
through your guidance, wisdom,
and the strength of your love,
    to become the person I am now.
I want you to know that
though I may not show it often enough,
you mean so much more to me
than words can say.
I thank you and I love you
with all my heart.

—Deanne Laura Gilbert

I have gone through
so many different stages
changing ideas and goals
while searching for the
right kind of life for me
You were always
ready to help me
at all times
It must have seemed like
I would never
follow one straight path

Now that I know
what I am doing and
where I am going
I can only show you
my extreme appreciation
for your support
by being true
to all the ideals and values
that you tried to teach me
Thank you forever
for standing by me
I love and appreciate
you forever

—Susan Polis Schutz

# I Love You, Dad

What can you say
to someone who has
always been one of
the most essential parts of your world;
someone who took you by the hand
  when you were little
and helped to show the way . . .

What do you say to someone
who stood by to help you grow,
providing love, strength, and support
so you could become the person
  you are today?

What can you say to let him know
that he's the best there is,
and that you hope you've inherited
  some of his wisdom and his strength?

What words would you say
  if you ever got the chance?

Maybe you just say
          "I love you, Dad . . ."

and hope he understands.

—Andrew Tawney

## You Have Given Me
## So Much More than You Know

I wish you could know
how much you have influenced my life.
You have shaped me as a human being,
making me the best I can be inside.
You have taught me wrong from right,
giving me room to experience things
    on my own.
You have nurtured me,
giving me love in your own special way,
whether it was a hug, a smile,
or a few quiet words of praise.

You have helped me
by giving me advice
on what you thought was right.
You have supported me by always
being there to help see me through.
You have shaped my morals and values
by passing things down that
could only come from you.
You have given me everything,
and by doing so,
I'm not only a part of you —
you've become a part of me.

—Stephanie Spilotro

## You Are the Best Father
## Anyone Ever Had

You're still the same dad
who meant the world to me
when I was little.

You're the same wonderful father
who took me by the hand when I
was little; the one who captured
my first smiles, my first steps, my
first everything with your camera.
You're the one who captured my heart
and encouraged my happiness
    every day of my life.
You're the one who watched me grow
and who always let me know
    how much I mattered to you.
You're the one who saw me go through
so many changes: from making messes
to making a difference,
from skinned knees and tears . . .
to every change the days and years
    have brought with them.

But there is one special change
that I don't think you're aware of yet,
and it's one that you deserve to know:

    It's that I thought I loved you
    with all my heart before . . .

    But now . . .
        I love you even more.

                            —Laurel Atherton

## I Feel So Lucky
## to Have You for My Father

You have given me so much
to be thankful for.
So much of who I am I owe to you,
and no matter where my life may
    take me,
a part of you is always with me.
I see a reflection of you
in all of my accomplishments,
and your support and love
always guide me.

You give me the ability
to see beauty in everything
    around me.
I can't thank you enough
for all that you've given me.
I couldn't have asked
for a more loving and special father.
I am the person that I am
    because of you,
and I am very proud to have you
in my life.

—Mary Renée Kunz

# I'll Always Love
## and Appreciate You

**D**ad, it is not always easy
to tell you how I feel about you.
I have left many of my thoughts unspoken,
thinking there would be another time,
a better time, to talk,
and yet time keeps passing by,
and it makes me realize
that the time is now
to let you know
how thankful I am for your love.
I appreciate you and respect you,
and though I don't tell you often,
I certainly feel it in my heart
always.

—Deanna Beisser

## I Have So Many Special
## Memories of You

I have a lot of special memories of you
tucked away in my heart.
Sometimes, I like to
take them out and remember
all the times you've been there
when I needed advice
and all the times you were silent
when I just needed to talk;
the many things you've done without
so I could have all the things I wanted;
letting me make my own decisions
without saying, "I told you so."

No matter how broken my heart,
you're always there to pick me up
and send me back into the world.
I remember all the things
you've done for me,
and I remember all the times
I took for granted:
all your love, all your support,
all your lost sleep, and
    all your worrying,
as well as all your smiles,
all your tears, all your help,
and all your advice.

I remember it all, Dad.
I'll never forget anything
    you've done.

—Patricia McGuire

## You Are a
## Very Special Father

It's true when they say
that anyone can be a father —
but it takes someone unique
and special to be the kind of
father you have been to me:
someone who shows me the
right way and yet guides me
to make my own way;
someone who has the time to care,
share, and listen;
and someone to correct me when
I'm wrong.
Although the differences
in our lives and in our times
are very obvious in some ways,
I want you to know
that you have loved me very well,
and my values are not really
so different from yours.

—Deena Rae McClure

23

What is a father?
A father is one of the most
   wonderful people in the world.

And though he rarely gets told that, it's true.
He's a man who, having been through childhood,
   youth, and adulthood himself,
can understand so many of the things
   his children go through in life.

He's good at providing direction and insight.
And when he does . . . it's all because
   his love and experience are shining through.
A father sacrifices, plans, strives, and achieves.
A father is someone who makes you believe
   in you.

A father is an essential man who never gets quite
   enough credit for the many contributions he
   makes to the family. As his father did for him,
   he will spend a lifetime trying to make
      life a little better than before.
   And he gives up some of his own dreams
      to make sure that some of yours come true.

A father is a very special man.
   He's a hand on your shoulder through
      every storm.
   His strength keeps you secure, and his love
      keeps you warm wherever you may go.

And if there is any way that he can be told . . .
   that he is loved, cherished, and thanked,
   then think of how much it would mean to him
   . . . if only he could know.

—Chris Gallatin

## Dear Dad . . .

I want you to know
that even though
my feelings somehow
   don't get spoken
      like they should,
the feelings are always
   warmly here,
      in my heart, for you.

And they would love
   to thank you
   for everything
      you are to me . . .
for everything you have done,
   and for every wonderful thing
      you continue to do.

   You're really something, Dad.

—Adrian Rogers

## You've Taught Me So Much Through Your Loving Example

You've made me proud to be myself.
From you, I have learned
that honesty is priceless and rare
and that wisdom and knowledge
are treasures that must be sought
throughout my life.
You've taught me that
to give and receive love
is the reward of living.

You've shown me that
words can encourage
a heart that's hurting.
You've shown me that w
are not necessarily spo
often they are expressed
by a silent look,
a caring touch,
or just a knowing between us.
You've taught me lessons
that are valuable
to living life successfully.
There's not a book
or school in the world
that could teach me
as well as you have
with the examples that
you have set before me.
Thank you for loving me,
for caring about me,
and for teaching me.

—Jewel Olson

## Thanks to You, Dad,
## I'm Making My Dreams Come True

I am where I am today
because of you.
Any dream I ever had,
no matter how big or how small,
grew when I shared it with you.
You encouraged me and taught me
that as long as I set my goals high
and tried my hardest to do my best,
anything was possible.
Your challenges
have made me a stronger person,
and because of you,
I know that no matter where I go,
I will always have my dreams.

—Lynn Brown

## I Will Always Be Grateful to You

In everyone's life,
there is a hero,
someone we admire
   and want to be like.
I know I haven't told you
often enough,
   but you are that person for me.
You have always been
a tower of strength
and inspiration in my life.
Even when I was struggling
with endless doubts
   and insecurities,
I never doubted
that I was truly loved.

Your love was always there —
in the faith you've had in me,
in the encouragement you gave
when I wished I could give up.
It showed in the sparkle
    in your eyes
when you supported my struggle
to become my own person,
always standing by when I needed
    your reassurance.
I will always be grateful
for your strong and sensitive
way of helping me become
    all that I am,
giving me the confidence
    to face the world.

—Melauni Lira

# Thank You, Dad

Thank you for always being there
every time I needed you.
Thank you for setting
a good example for me
and guiding me in the right direction.
Thank you for not giving up on me
when it looked like I might be
headed in the wrong direction.
Thank you for listening to me and
actually caring about what I had to say.
Thank you for saying "no"
to the things I wanted to do
that weren't in my best interests.
Thank you for saying "yes"
to the things that have enhanced
my growth as an individual.
Thank you for the unconditional love
you expressed to me throughout the years.
It is only through your type of love
that children and their parents
form a unique bond that will never part.

—Bill Crowley

I was given a gift
by being born into a family of love —
a caring family that has been guided
   by you.
With wise principles put before me,
you have taught me how to take
the most productive paths in my life.
Through your love,
you've given me warmth,
security, and stability,
helping me achieve the
most out of life,
and letting me see how wonderful
the world can be.
From a solid upbringing,
I have found strength —
a source of power that I draw from
to manage my life.

You have a special talent
that has made you such a wonderful father.
I credit you with my well-being,
and I thank you
from deep within my heart.

—Sandra Mooney

## This Is My Promise to You

I promise that I will always try
to be the best person that I can be —
someone you can always be proud of.
I will strive to be honest at all times
and to be a gentle, loving,
and forgiving person
who can always be counted on.
I promise that I will always
respect you and your opinions,
and I will listen to your advice
with an open mind.
I will hold tightly to the beliefs
and values that you have instilled in me.
I will never give up on any of my dreams.
I will believe in myself and my abilities,
just as you always have.
And I also promise that
you will forever be an important part
of my life.

—Deanne Laura Gilbert

# I'm Glad You're
# My Dad

When I was little,
I was so impressed by your
strength and intelligence.
I used to think there was nothing
that you couldn't fix, or any
problem that you couldn't solve.

Now that I'm grown and on my own,
I still carry with me
the values that you instilled.
I also carry with me the memories
of our special times together
and the feelings of the wonderful
kind of love that a child
feels for a father.

I still look to you for that
strength and wisdom that I so
admired as a little child,
and I want you to know
that in my eyes
you will always be the most
wonderful dad in the world.

—Ginny Dugger

# A Family Is Love

... and I Want You to Know
that I Think I Have the
Best Family in the World

A family
sees each other
in every living situation
in every emotion
in every mood
and still stands beside each other
A family
cries and laughs together
and helps each other
through sickness to health
throughout their lives
A family
cares for their young and old
with all their love and effort
A family
provides values and morals
and arrives at a standard for living
A family
hugs each other with tears
when one member leaves home
and gives each other  courage and strength
to come back
A family
works towards the same goals
helping each other to succeed
at all times
A family
is happy for one another when something
    great happens
and cries for one another  when something
    sad happens

A family
travels together, plays together
learns together, grows up together
and interacts with society
in every way
together
A family
shares the same history
and an understanding of each other
that helps them
to better understand themselves and the world
A family
has holidays and rituals
that bring them close together
in a very happy way
A family
has bonds which
can never be broken
and which can give strength to each other
in order to help them survive
A family
has unconditional love for one another
forever
and I want you to know
that I think I have
the best family
in the world

—Susan Polis Schutz

## Every Day I Am Thankful
## to Have You for My Father

For all you've given me,
for all you've taught me,
and for every time you've helped me,
I think of how very fortunate I am.
I think of how we've both done
our share of growing over the years,
and only now have we come to realize
what a good friend we have in each other.
We're so very much alike,
and I think that's why
it has sometimes been difficult for us,
but I also think that's why
we're so close.

I love having you to turn to,
and I want you to know
that I'm here for you, too.
For all my life,
for the happy memories,
the lessons learned,
the chance to be myself,
and for being such a wonderful father,
I thank you with all my heart,
and I love you with all that I am.

—Julia Baron Alvarez

## You've Been a Really
## Great Teacher . . .

You've taught me so much,
and you've taught me well.
The things that I've learned from you
are the most valuable I'll ever possess.
By loving me, you taught me how to love;
by trusting me, you taught me to trust;
by having faith in me,
    you taught me to have faith;
and by respecting me, you taught me respect.
From you, I've learned what it is
to be  forgiven and how to forgive
myself as well as others.
I've learned that the greatest gifts come
from giving of ourselves,
and that those who receive gifts graciously
and appreciate them fully
have already given something in return.
You've taught me to be patient, to accept
things, and to appreciate each new day.

You've taught me to help others freely
and to ask for help just as freely.
You've taught me the value of hard work
and of the necessity to play and enjoy life.
You've taught me to strive for what I want
and for what I believe in and to look
at things through the eyes of others,
not just my own.
You've taught me not to judge this world
or the people in it, and that we alone are
the best judges of ourselves.
You've taught me the value of imagination,
education, and natural curiosity.
You've taught me that the very best way
to live life is by learning about it.
You are a wonderful parent
and the best teacher I'll ever know.

—Karen Poynter Taylor

I wish there were a way
to repay you
for all that you've done for me:
all the caring, all the love,
all the sacrifice and concern.
I always knew
you would be there for me,
and that your love never depended
on what I did or didn't do.
You encouraged me to work towards
and reach whatever goals I set,
and you helped me to have faith
in my abilities.
You taught me that mistakes
don't mean failure,
only that I need to try harder.
Thank you for all these things,
and for everything that made
my growing-up years a very
    special time.

—M. Joye

### Here Are Seven Reasons Why
### It's Great to Have You for My Father

— You are the best father
anyone could ever hope to have.
— Your wonderful qualities have made
a lasting impression on me that I
will admire for as long as I live.
— You give me so much to be thankful for.
— You have wisdom that goes beyond
your words, a sweetness that goes
beyond your smile, and a heart
of pure gold.

— You take the time to hear my deepest
   thoughts, my feelings, and my fears.
— You've dried tears no one else could see,
   you've helped me find happiness,
     and you've taught me that I really can
        make some of my dreams come true.
— There isn't a child in all
   the world who could ask for
      a more wonderful father . . . than you.

                                   —Chris Gallatin

## You Are Everything
## a Father Should Be

A father is a guide on the
journey to adulthood,
a teacher of morals and values.
He listens to problems
and helps to find their solutions.
He is a friend, always there
to share the good and the bad.
He is someone who gets respect
because he deserves it,
trust because he earns it,
and love because of all he is.

—M. Joye

## For All
### that You Are to Me, Dad . . .

There have been times
in my life when I've wanted
to express my feelings,
but I let the chances
   slip by.
There have been times
when I've been grateful
for your wisdom
and thankful
for your unending faith in me,
but didn't let you know.

We may not have always agreed
on every issue,
but now I see that you
were using your past experiences
to guide me in the best way
that you knew how,
and that you had only
good things in mind.
I've missed some opportunities
to tell you my feelings,
so I want you to know now
that I love you
and appreciate you.
Thank you for all
you've ever been to me.

—Jane Pofahl

**A**s I was growing up,
I didn't always realize
everything you did for me.
I didn't always know or understand
the way you thought.
Yet you waited patiently
and gave me room to grow.
You let me make my own decisions,
and when they were wrong,
you picked me up
and encouraged me to try again.

So many years have passed
since I was a child,
and now I realize that
all the little things you did for me
were your way of showing that
    you loved me.
I've grown so much since then,
but I'll never be too big to say. . .
"I love you, Dad."

—John B. Kalusa

## Dad, This Is What I Mean
## Every Time I Tell You that I Love You

So many times I've wanted to tell you
   everything I feel for you.
Usually, I simply say, "I love you,"
but I've always wanted to say more,
because somehow those words
   just don't seem to be enough.

I want to tell you how much respect and
   admiration I have for you.
I want to tell you that I notice
   how hard you work and how,
no matter how tired you are,
you never fail to be there for me
   when I need you most.
I want to let you know that
the many things you've given up for me
   haven't gone unnoticed.

It was you who said
I could be whatever I wanted to be
   and to never settle for less.
It was you who taught me to love myself
   before I could give love to another.
It was you who taught me to be proud,
to love with true devotion,
and to give of myself to those in need.
But most of all,
you taught me to dream
   with the universe as my boundary,
to reach for my goals
   with the sky as my limit,
and to take failure as a foundation
   for growth.

Dad, I don't know if I'll ever be able
   to express all that I feel for you.
But I hope you know what I mean
   every time I say, "I love you."

—Kathryn Lestelle

# This Is for You, Dad . . .

This is for you:
for the one who has cared
all these years
but has never heard enough
about how much I care . . .

This is for someone who is
a wonderful example
of what more people should be.

For the person whose devotion
to his family is marked by
gentle guidance, and whose
love of life, sense of direction,
and down-to-earth wisdom
make more sense to me now
than nearly any other thing
I've learned.

If you never knew how much
I love and respect you,
I want you to know it now, Dad . . .

Because I think that
you're the best father
any child ever had.

—Adrian Rogers

**I** am your child.

And that — to me — is one of
the most wonderful things
anyone could ever
  hope to be.

I am someone who loves you more
than words can say.
I am the one you helped
every step of the way
along the path of life.

Your love was always there
    to brighten up my world;
your wisdom was there to help me learn.
Your patience and care were always there
    to see me through all those difficult days
    of growing up.
And your sweetness and smiles
were always there to make the path
as smooth as possible for me.

You have given so much that I can never repay.
Thinking of it all makes me well up with tears
    that are overflowing with happiness
        and appreciation and thanks.
And I would give anything
if you knew how very much
    I'll always love you, Dad.

—Laurel Atherton

# ACKNOWLEDGMENTS

The following is a partial list of authors whom the publisher especially wishes to thank for permission to reprint their works.

Patricia McGuire for "I Have So Many Special Memories of You."

Deena Rae McClure for "You Are a Very Special Father."

Jewel Olson for "You've Taught Me So Much Through Your Loving Example."

Lynn Brown for "Thanks to You, Dad, I'm Making My Dreams Come True."

Melauni Lira for "I Will Always Be Grateful to You."

Sandra Mooney for "I was given a gift . . ."

Deanne Laura Gilbert for "This Is My Promise to You."

Ginny Dugger for "I'm Glad You're My Dad."

Karen Poynter Taylor for "You've Been a Really Great Teacher . . ."

**Broward Sheriff's Office**
2601 W. Broward Blvd.
Fort Lauderdale, FL 33312

# Citizen Observer Patrol

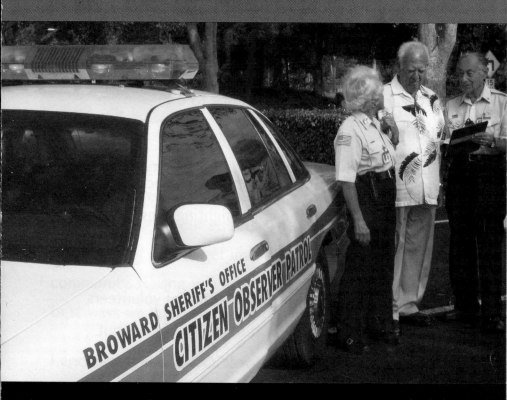

C    potassium

B

Folic acid  Calcium

B12    magnesium

E + C

Bilberry   meal replacement

Chro. Mag.

gingo biloba  protein

DHEA   Banana

    supplements 110/70

   no smoke
   no drink